ONE HUNGRY DRAGON

To Amelie, who fixed the ending - A.C.

For Dara and Walter - A.W.

HODDER CHILDREN'S BOOKS
First published in Great Britain in 2023
by Hodder and Stoughton

10 9 8 7 6 5 4 3 2 1

Text © Alastair Chisholm, 2023
Illustrations © Alex Willmore, 2023

The moral rights of the author and illustrator
have been asserted. All rights reserved.

A CIP catalogue record for this book
is available from the British Library.

HB ISBN 978 1 44496 659 6
PB ISBN 978 1 44496 660 2

Printed and bound in China

MIX
Paper from
responsible sources
FSC® C104740
FSC
www.fsc.org

HODDER CHILDREN'S BOOKS
An imprint of Hachette
Children's Group
Part of Hodder and Stoughton
Carmelite House, 50 Victoria
Embankment, London EC4Y 0DZ

An Hachette UK Company
www.hachette.co.uk
www.hachettechildrens.co.uk

Alastair Chisholm and Alex Willmore

ONE HUNGRY DRAGON

Hodder Children's Books

Deep in a dark and gloomy forest,
a creature stomps through the trees.
"I am Bernardo," he roars, "and I am
ONE HUNGRY DRAGON!

A-ha!" he says. "What's this?"

It's TWO silly sheep,
grazing in the meadow.

Bernardo gobbles them up in a great big gulp!

"Delicious!" growls Bernardo, licking his lips.
But he is still **ONE HUNGRY DRAGON!**

"A-ha! What's this?"

It's THREE hearty heroes, valiant and bold!
"Begone, foul beast!" they cry.

"Foul? ME?" roars Bernardo. "How rude!"
He melts their swords with his fiery breath . . .

. . . and swallows
the heroes whole!

But Bernardo is still
ONE HUNGRY
DRAGON.

"A-ha! What's this?"

Here come **FOUR proper princesses,** brave and true.

"Stop this right now, you dreadful dragon! We're not afraid of you!"

"You should be afraid," huffs Bernardo. "**Watch!**"

ONE (gulp).

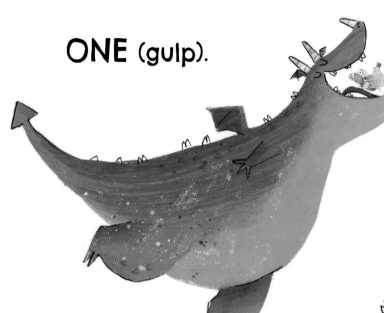

TWO (gulp).

THREE (gulp).

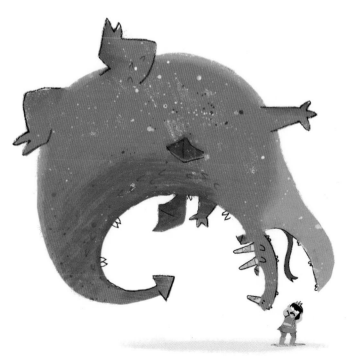

FOUR (gulp)!
But Bernardo is still
ONE HUNGRY DRAGON.

"A-ha! What's this?"

Here are **FIVE** frisky foxes,
who dart and dodge and dive!
"You can't escape!" Bernardo laughs.
"I'm the fastest thing alive!"

He flings them up and
gobbles them down.
"Hee-hee,
tickly tails!"

Now look!
SIX bristly bears,
furious and fierce.
"You're not as fierce as me!"
growls Bernardo.
"ROOOOOAAAARRRRRR!"

And what's this?
SEVEN magical mermaids
in an underwater world.

"Mmmm! Salty snacks!"
laughs Bernardo.

Sluuuuuurp!

But Bernardo is *still*
ONE HUNGRY DRAGON.

And so... EIGHT funny frogs - hop, hop, hop!

NINE fairy godmothers - flutter, flutter, flutter!

TEN little piggies - trot, trot, trot!
All into Bernardo's great big mouth!

"Deeeeee-licious," sighs Bernardo at last.
"Now I am **ONE VERY FULL** dragon!"

And with a great big
s-t-r-e-t-c-h
and a mighty **YAWN,**
he curls up and
starts to snore.

"WE know what to do,"
say the princesses.

"On your marks . . . get set . . . jump!"

Bernardo wakes up. He feels very strange.

"Oi!" he grumbles.

"What's going on in there?"

Jump-jump-jump! Bounce-

bounce-**bounce!** Hop-**hop**-hop!

"**Stop that!**" moans Bernardo.
"I don't feel very well." He hiccups, and then . . .

pppppppppp!"

"Run!" shout the princesses.

TEN little piggies - trot, trot, trot!
NINE fairy godmothers -
flutter, flutter, "Bye!"

EIGHT funny frogs – hoppity-hop-hop!
SEVEN magic mermaids – splish, splash, dive!
SIX bristly bears – stomp, stomp, stomp!

FIVE frisky foxes – jump, jump, jump!

FOUR proper princesses – "Quick, quick, quick!"

THREE hearty heroes – puff, puff, puff!

TWO silly sheep – baa, baa, baa!

All out of Bernardo's mouth!

"Urgh . . ." moans Bernardo.

"Bernardo, that was
very naughty!"
says the biggest princess.

"I'm sorry," Bernardo wails.
"But I'm hungry!"

"Well . . ." says the second princess. "Would you like to come back for a feast with us?"

Bernardo gasps. "Really?"

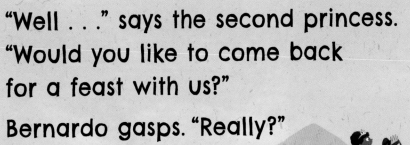

"Only if you promise to be good!" say the smaller princesses.

"Oh, I promise!" says Bernardo.

So the princesses invite everyone to their castle – even Bernardo . . .

. . . who is **ONE HAPPY DRAGON!**

The End.

(But what's this?)